WIZARD BEANO & PALS

Written by Paula Fowler   Illustrated by Kylie Dixon

Dedicated to all my family, friends and of course Harry x

First Published by Compass-Publishing UK 2023
ISBN 978-1-915962-01-0

Text © Paula Fowler, 2023
Illustrations © Kylie Dixon, 2023

Edited by Alexa Tewkesbury
Typeset by The Book Refinery Ltd
www.TheBookRefinery.com

THIS BOOK BELONGS TO

....

MEET JOE & JOE

Joe Senior is the creator of Wizard Beano, and the artwork by Kylie Dixon
that became the inspiration for this book was commissioned as a gift for baby Joe.

WIZARD BEANO & PALS

Before I begin, let me explain who Wizard Beano is and how his story has played a huge part in the lives of the Fowler family.

The family home, in Hastings Hill, Sunderland, always bubbled with life, mainly due to the antics of Gill, Alison and Jeff.

But there was a special time every day when the boisterous noise became a hushed buzz of excitement. This was right before bedtime, when Joseph – Joe – would settle down and tell his children a bedtime story: a Wizard Beano adventure!

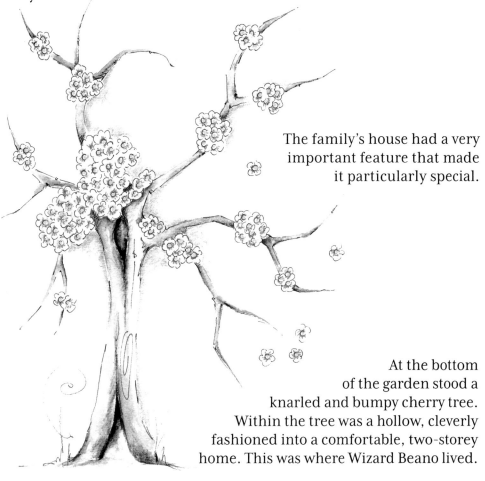

The family's house had a very important feature that made it particularly special.

At the bottom of the garden stood a knarled and bumpy cherry tree. Within the tree was a hollow, cleverly fashioned into a comfortable, two-storey home. This was where Wizard Beano lived.

Wizard Beano was, by name and nature, a wizard. However, to some who heard about him, he was much, much more than that. He was a friend and a member of the family who was, and still is, held permanently in their hearts.

Wizard Beano was only a little fellow. You could literally carry him around with you in your hand or your backpack, or he might sit quite comfortably on your shoulder.

From toe to head, he was exceptionally smart. He was always to be seen dressed in black boots with shiny buckles. That sheen was something he was very proud of. His red coat was beautifully tailored, if a little worn at the elbows, and had very prominent buttons. Underneath, he wore black velvet trousers that fell to just below the knee, and a crisp, white shirt. All this was topped off with a black, pointed hat, which was sometimes a little crooked and seemed to have a life of its own. What made the hat special was that, occasionally, it twinkled, due to the stars which clung to the fabric.

But perhaps the most unusual thing about Wizard Beano was the fact that not everyone could see him. Grown-up humans – most of them, at least – simply weren't able to. Their eyes were far too unbelieving.

Children and other creatures, however, had kinder, more forgiving eyes. So not only could these clever ones see Wizard Beano, they could speak to him too.

Wizard Beano had a special gift: he knew instinctively when and where he was needed, and he had the ability to get there, at high speed, whenever required – often, using just a little bit magic.

As Joe's bedtime stories unfolded, Gill, Alison and Jeff were able to spend lots of time with the wizard. They shared his adventures, helped to solve problems and, on occasion, got into mischief.

The years went by, and, as Gill, Alison and Jeff grew up, Joe became Grandad Joe, and Wizard Beano and all his antics were introduced to the grandchildren. James, Ben, Jessica, Alex, Beth and Sam would listen, eyes wide and mouths open in anticipation, when they visited Gran and Grandad Joe.

As more time passed and the grandchildren grew older too, the Fowler family had fewer and fewer opportunities to bring Wizard Beano to life. But don't worry – he was still talked about at family get-togethers and, as I've mentioned, he was always in our memories and close to our hearts.

Then, one day, came an exciting moment for the whole family: in 2021, the first great-grandchild made an entrance – Joseph Junior.

The question was, could Great-Grandad Joe still remember Wizard Beano?

Silly question – of course he could! And when everyone's memories had been jogged, we made sure to check with Wizard Beano himself that he could let us know what he'd been up to over the last few years.

Well – did he have some tales to tell!

So, are you ready? Then let the new adventures begin!

CHARLIE MEETS WIZARD BEANO

The wind howled loudly. As multi-coloured leaves swirled around the street in Hastings Hill, the gnarled and bumpy cherry tree swayed.

Charlie clung to the branch but could feel their fingertips slowly losing their grip. This was the worst storm there had been in a very long time. It looked as though the tree, which had been Charlie's home for over a year, wouldn't last the night.

Charlie had already been looking for a new place to live and this was definitely the right time to move. Fortunately, there were a few other cherry trees nearby that were still standing strong and straight. They just refused to let the gusts bend them.

Peering in through the front window of a house close to one of the trees, Charlie saw that a family lived there. There was noise and laughter and Charlie felt a warm feeling inside. Moving to the garden here would be an excellent idea. He'd have a new family to be part of.

Yes, this is it, Charlie thought. *Perfect.*

Battling the high winds and the beginnings of a nasty storm, Charlie gradually moved all their possessions. Backwards and forwards they went, from the fragile, wind-torn tree where they'd been living, to a cosy, dry hollow in the much sturdier, upright tree in the family's garden. One part of the hollow even seemed to have a ready-formed wardrobe for all their belongings.

When all the items had finally been moved, Charlie was extremely tired and a little tearful. Falling, exhausted, into the hollow of the tree, they landed in the huge pile of clothes, boots, shoes and lots of bits and bobs ...

Early the next morning, Wizard Beano opened his eyes and stretched. He always woke as the sun came up and the birds started to sing. That was his alarm clock. It had been incredibly windy through the night but that hadn't stopped him from sleeping.

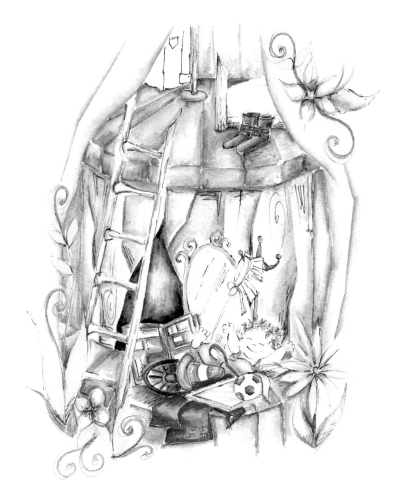

Little did Wizard Beano know, however, that he had a visitor. Not only that, the only space the visitor hadn't taken up was the small room where the wizard stood right now.

Wizard Beano found his shirt and trousers, got dressed as he always did and went to fetch his beautifully tailored red coat, his black, pointed hat with the stars on the fabric, and, of course, his wand.

Climbing down the wooden ladder, Wizard Beano was still bleary-eyed from sleep. Again, as he did every morning, he stretched towards the peg where his coat always hung. Then he felt around for it with his outstretched hand.

That's when he started to wake up properly. His coat wasn't there. Instead, he grabbed a piece of fabric and was shocked to find he was holding a white, frilly net skirt!

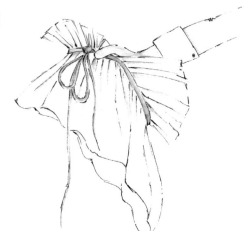

'Hi ...' said a small voice. 'My name's Charlie. May I please have my tutu?' Charlie looked at the bewildered expression on Wizard Beano's face.

'Your *what?*' Wizard Beano exclaimed, in what can only be described as a high-pitched screech. 'What are you doing in my house? And where is my coat?'

'Please don't be cross,' said Charlie quietly. 'I didn't think you'd mind.'

Of course, Wizard Beano didn't know that Charlie's home had been destroyed in the storm. He didn't realise poor Charlie had only just managed to move their belongings, before the wind and the rain had snapped the trunk of the tree where they'd been living. He had no idea that, where Charlie's bedroom had been, there was now just a huge hole.

But Wizard Beano had been alone in the cherry tree for so long that the sight of Charlie was a huge shock.

'I'm sorry I screamed,' said the wizard. He still looked angry but his eyes had softened a little. 'Please find me my coat. Then you can tell me what's happened.'

He watched Charlie disappear under the pile of belongings, until a hand suddenly popped out with a red coat attached to it.

'Ta-da!' Charlie sang, as their face popped out too.

It looked very happy.

Wizard Beano put on his coat, then pointed outside to a flat seating area on a thick branch.

As they sat there together, Charlie explained to him about the scary and terrible night they had had: how difficult it had been to carry everything; how he'd had to fight against the wind. And as Wizard Beano listened, he felt a little sorry for his new friend.

'Very well,' he agreed at last, although he did sound a little reluctant. 'You may move in. But I do have rules and they must be followed.' Charlie nodded. 'Of course,' they said, and the rules were written on a scroll. But secretly, Charlie knew following the rules was going to be difficult. Choosing the right outfit in the morning was something that needed a lot of thought. Sometimes, it took at least four or five different combinations before Charlie could decide on one and was ready to set out. This might mean it was mid-morning before they left home. Which also meant they often missed the opportunity to play with friends or even eat breakfast.

Rules
1. All clutter must be kept tidy.
2. The timetable must be kept to:
   Get up, get washed and dressed at sunrise. Set out early on adventures with the whole day ahead.

As the untidy heap of clothes, accessories, boots and shoes started to shrink while Charlie filled the wardrobe, they muttered, 'But I can do this ... I can ...'

OVER THE RAINBOW

The clouds started to change colour. What had been a beautiful day, with blue skies as far as the eye could see, suddenly became dark. The air felt damp and heavy.

More than twenty young rabbits raced across the grass hill to the shelter of their burrows, with the shadow from Penshaw monument behind them.

But two of them still played happily. They hid in the long grass. They raced each other from one tree to the next. They hadn't noticed the rainbow arching overhead, or the big raindrops that looked like Christmas tree baubles. The drops fell through the coloured stripes of light and hit the ground with a splash.

When at last the two bunnies realised the weather had turned, they dashed back to their burrow, getting drenched by the heavy shower. They were extremely wet when they got there, but at least they were just in time for some supper.

Afterwards, they snuggled together and quickly dropped off to sleep. They dreamt of carrots and lettuce, which they hoped to get from the local garden centre the following day.

Meanwhile, back at Hastings Hill, Wizard Beano and Charlie sat on the branch of the cherry tree, looking at the beautiful rainbow. Dark grey sky stretched away on one side and bright blue on the other.

Wizard Beano had noticed flashes of colour as the rain fell over Penshaw monument.

'It's magical, Charlie,' he said, and he looked up into the sky. 'I have a very funny feeling about tonight. Let's go out early tomorrow morning. Please choose an outfit now.'

'Really?' Charlie replied. 'But I don't even know what the weather's going to be like tomorrow.'

Before Charlie knew it, however, it all seemed to be agreed. So Charlie thought about it, and decided the best option would be to choose something to wear now, and perhaps take a raincoat or an umbrella too.

Wizard Beano nodded his head. 'Hmm,' he said to himself, looking pleased. 'We're making progress with this one.'

The following morning, back in the burrow, the two young rabbits stirred and stretched themselves. When they're eyes were properly open, they were surprised to see all the other rabbits from the burrow staring at them.

They were even more surprised when, one by one, the onlookers scurried away. None of them seemed quite sure what to say. As they disappeared, their whispers became giggles. Then their giggles exploded into laughter.

'Did you see the boys?' they shrieked. 'What's happened to Raine? Those ears! And did you see Beau's tail ...?!'

The two bunny friends who were still in their beds rubbed their eyes and wondered why the others had left them.

All at once – 'Oh ... oh, no!' cried Raine. 'Look at your tail, Beau ...'

But Beau was already glaring at Raine's ears. What on earth had happened?

The two rabbits hurried out of the burrow – and stared at each other.

Raine had a rainbow-coloured tail.

Beau had rainbow colours all over the insides of his ears.

The pair frantically rubbed their fur on the grass, still damp from the storm the evening before. But no matter how much they rubbed, the rainbow colours seemed there to stay.

After a while, Raine and Beau felt tummy rumbles and realised how hungry they were. So they went to join their friends and find some juicy leaves to eat.

But – 'We're not standing near you,' some of the other rabbits said. They were so rude. 'You're different from us. We don't want to catch your rainbow colours. Go away!'

This went on day after day.

Raine and Beau were sad the other rabbits didn't want to be their friends anymore. But they quickly got used to having just each other for company. They even found a comfy place under a log in the woods, where they could make a new home.

The rabbits had to share the woods with lots of other animals, and with birds and humans too. They often saw families climb up to Penshaw monument. Then they'd watch them go to have a snack in the garden centre below and walk through the woods to look at the beautiful scenery.

But some people travelled to this beautiful place by car, which caused problems for the animals. To reach the delicious foods at the garden centre – salad leaves, carrots, radishes – they had to cross the busy road.

One particular day, Wizard Beano and Charlie were out exploring, when they heard a dreadful cry coming from the side of the road at the bottom of the footpath.

'Help! Please, HELP!'

To their horror, they could see a rabbit lying on the roadside. She was struggling even to call out. The effort to shout seemed really painful for her.

'Oh, no!' said Charlie. 'That poor rabbit!'

'Please find my babies,' the rabbit pleaded. 'I was hit by a car and thrown across the road. I remember telling my babies to run to the burrow and stay there until I get back. But I can't move.' Her eyes glazed over.

I'm not going to get back to the burrow, she thought. Tears fell down her cheeks and Wizard Beano and Charlie heard a tiny sob.

Wizard Beano wished he knew a magic spell to help her. But all he could do was hope they'd be able to help in some other way.

'Where have your children gone?' Charlie asked. 'Where's the burrow?' He leaned forward so that he could hear the rabbit's reply.

Mammy rabbit managed to give some directions.

Then, 'Don't you worry,' Charlie said. 'I'll find it.'

With that, Charlie rushed away up the hill, around the monument and into the woods beyond.

Wizard Beano stayed behind and gently stroked the mammy rabbit's ear to try to make her comfortable. 'Charlie will find your family,' he said, 'and make sure they're safe.'

Charlie rushed into the woods. As they hurried by, they couldn't help but notice two rabbits sitting under a log. What stood out was their brightly coloured tail and ears, but Charlie quickly put that to the back of their mind.

'I have to find the babies,' Charlie said, breathless from running.

Following the mammy rabbit's instructions, they soon found the burrow. Little white whiskers and pink noses peeked out.

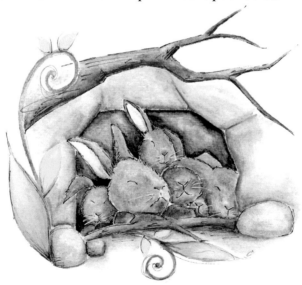

Charlie counted. 'One, two, three, four, five, six. Yep, all there. Phew. Now, you must stay here,' Charlie ordered the little bundles of light brown fluff, in a stern voice. 'It's very important that you do.'

With those words, Charlie galloped away, back through the woods and down the steep hill, practically flying through the air.

'Did you find them?' Wizard Beano asked. 'Are they safe?'

'Yes,' Charlie said, reaching the place where the little ones' mam lay.

'Thank you.' The injured rabbit looked calmer. 'Please tell my babies I love them very much. And please take care of them.'

Charlie nodded, although they didn't really understand what she meant.

As the beautiful mammy rabbit closed her eyes for the last time, all the pain went away. She smiled and relaxed, knowing now that someone would take care of her children. Then she went peacefully to sleep.

 HAPPY FAMILIES

One day, a scream filled the air. It was so loud, it felt as though it could be heard across the whole of Penshaw and beyond. What had been a quiet, peaceful morning in the woods turned to chaos.

'I am not taking care of these bunnies anymore!' Charlie bellowed at Wizard Beano. 'Can't you use your magic on them? You're supposed to be a wizard! I turn one way and I lose one bunny. Just as I get them all together again, another one runs off. I'm tired and I'm fed up. All I want is a wash and to put on a new outfit and get away from these monsters!'

And Charlie screamed again.

Wizard Beano looked at the sweet-looking, fluffy bunnies and wondered how difficult it could be.

'Don't worry, Charlie,' he said. 'I'll take over for a bit, if you like. You have some time for yourself.'

Before the wizard could change his mind, Charlie ran off. They were beginning to think that looking after the orphaned family really wasn't for them.

But then Charlie remembered the promise they'd made to the bunnies' wonderful mam at the side of the road. Somehow, they'd have to keep it. They just weren't sure how.

Once at the cherry tree, Charlie changed into a pretty, lilac tunic. It felt calming to put on a fresh outfit. Feeling more relaxed, they then began to think of ways to entertain the lively baby bunnies.

As Charlie wandered back through the woods, they noticed the two rainbow rabbits they'd seen before. There they were again next to the log. Both looked deep in conversation, but they seemed a little frustrated and sad.

One of them suddenly began to sob. 'I want to be part of something bigger, Beau,' he cried. 'I want to have babies and be a real family.'

The other shook his head. 'But, Raine, you know that's not possible for us.'

Charlie could hardly believe his ears. Hcre was an opportunity too good to miss.

'Follow me!' Charlie called.

Raine glanced up at the lilac tunic, wafting in the breeze. 'I suppose we may as well,' he said, giving Beau a nudge. 'Better than sitting here moping.'

When the three of them arrived at the baby bunnies' burrow, they found Wizard Beano snoozing. Six bundles of fluff were gathered round him.

Don't know what all the fuss was about, the wizard had thought to himself. *This is easy.* He had, however, resorted to using just a little magic to give his tired old legs a rest. The special word, 'Abracadabra', had left his lips only moments ago.

'Ta-da!' Charlie sang. 'Raine – Beau – meet your new family!'

Before Raine and Beau had the chance to ask any questions, Charlie grabbed Wizard Beano's arm.

'Quick!' Charlie pulled the wizard's red coat sleeve, propelling them both down the hill. 'Don't look back!'

As Wizard Beano stumbled after Charlie, he felt very confused. 'But what's going on?'

'It's simple!' Charlie shouted, still hurtling down the grassy bank. 'I've found new parents for the bunnies!'

Charlie kept pulling Wizard Beano along, so he didn't get the chance to object.

It was only when they were nearly back at the cherry tree that Charlie explained. 'Raine and Beau want a family and can't have one. You have lots of adventures and I have places to be, so we have very little time. It's a perfect fix for the puzzle!'

Wizard Beano went off for a sleep and a ponder. *It does make sense*, he thought to himself. *But is it too easy?*

A day later, he and Charlie went back into the woods. They knew it was important to make sure the little bunnies were all right.

There, they found all six young rabbits playing happily. Raine and Beau looked happy too. They smiled and played along with their very own family.

Wizard Beano looked pleased. 'Well done, Charlie,' he said with a smile when they got back to Hastings Hill. 'Now, off you go to choose an outfit for tomorrow. It'll save time in the morning and we have things to do.'

'Ugh, this is so difficult,' Charlie groaned to himself. But, if they were to remain in the comfy cherry tree, they knew it had to be done. After all, rules were rules.

DIABLO, THE 'HANGRY' WIZARD

Diablo was a young boy who loved trying out magic tricks. He was always on the go.

Most mornings, Diablo got quickly out of bed, then hurried to have a wash. Well ... perhaps 'wash' doesn't really describe it. Using a damp cloth, he would rub in a small, circular movement around his face. Then he'd brush perhaps one or two teeth and pat his hair down. This was quickly followed by pulling on a hat – a beanie. But it wasn't an ordinary beanie. Whenever he performed his spells, he could turn it into a pointy wizard's hat.

Diablo's mam and dad were often already at work by the time he got out of bed. Mam was a nurse and Dad had a job that meant he was out very early each morning. But Diablo didn't really know what he did.

On weekdays at school, Diablo found he got frustrated. Nothing seemed to make sense. He spent most of his time feeling angry and upset.

But weekends – now, they were a different story. Freedom! Diablo loved being outside and not being made to sit in one place for what seemed like hours at a time.

The one thing Diablo loved to do more than anything else, however, was magic! He would practise every possible second he could.

He even tried to entertain the other school children with his magic tricks. But they would often laugh when he got something wrong and he'd grow flustered. His cheeks would turn red with embarrassment and his hands would shake.

Often, the more he tried, the more mistakes he made. Some of the kids would form a circle round him, which made him feel even more under pressure; even more likely to fail. Beads of sweat would form on the back of his neck, and his hands would turn clammy.

'Why can I do this trick at home and not here?' he said under his breath one day at school. He'd practised all lunchtime and missed yet another meal, because he'd forgotten to stand in the lunch queue.

That made afternoon lessons worse. His tummy rumbled and he couldn't focus because he was sleepy.

'Wake up, Diablo,' said Mr Smith, the maths teacher, in a stern voice.

Oh, no, Diablo thought. *I'm in trouble again.*

Thankfully, it was the end of the week and he already knew what he was going to do on Saturday morning ...

Diablo got very little sleep that night. However, he was still full of energy when he got out of bed, fuelled by excitement – it was the weekend after all. Super happy, he raced out through the front door.

His mam called, 'Diablo! You haven't had breakfast!'

Diablo took no notice and continued to run towards the swimming baths.

The Aquatic Centre was new. It was a beautiful swimming pool next to the Stadium of Light football ground. All his school friends went swimming there on a Saturday morning.

As Diablo arrived, his black coat wafting like a cape behind him, he froze to the spot. The boys who had ridiculed him at school the day before stood in the doorway. They glared at him and laughed.

His mouth went dry. He couldn't speak out loud and the hairs on the back of his neck tingled.

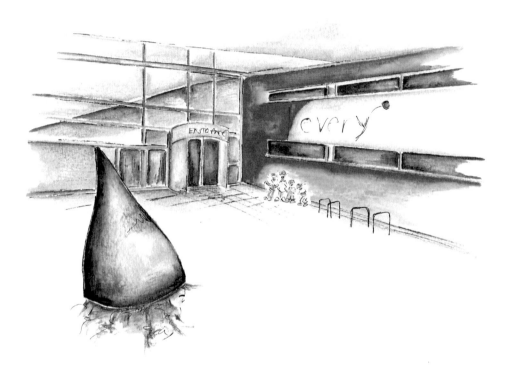

Why did he always feel like this?

Diablo grew angry, although more with himself than with anyone else. He quickly turned his beanie into the pointy wizard hat. Then, muttering a spell under his breath, he whispered, 'I'll teach you!' And he tapped his spell book, which was very well hidden in the inside pocket of his cape. He'd been waiting for this opportunity: he was going to glue the bully boys to the ground so they'd feel the way he did when they ridiculed him.

At least, that's what
the spell said would happen.

From outside the Aquatic Centre,
Diablo could see the pool through the
big window. All of a sudden, the kids who
were swimming there started to scream.
The water in the pool had begun to thicken and stick
to the children's bodies, and it had turned a purply-pink colour.

The lifeguards on the side of the pool glanced at each other. 'It looks like jelly,' one of them said.

He noticed a girl trying to climb out of the pool, with the gunge sticking to her legs. 'It is jelly,' he said. 'Sticky, thick, gloopy raspberry jelly.'

Diablo gasped. 'Oh, no ...' he muttered, and began frantically searching through his spell book to reverse what he'd done.

But what he'd failed to realise was that the first spell had gone wrong. So no matter how many times he tapped the book, scratched his head, read the page, chanted different words and shouted out spells – nothing would work.

Everyone at the pool stared and glared and wondered what had happened. Poor Diablo, meanwhile, sneaked into the Aquatic Centre to hide behind the reception desk. He wished he could transport himself far away.

Some way off, in Hastings Hill, Wizard Beano and Charlie had already heard the children's screams. They echoed along the River Wear all the way to the cherry tree.

'Someone needs help!' exclaimed Wizard Beano. 'And they need it now!'

The wizard grabbed Charlie's hand, and up and away they flew.

Over the Spire Bridge with its fine wire and clean lines.

Over the top of the Stadium of Light.

Charlie thought the view was fabulous, but there was no time for sightseeing.

As the two of them arrived, Wizard Beano could feel the magic in the air. He could also sense where the mistake had been made.

The wizard didn't have to look far to spot a broken wand next to a black cloak, in a quiet corner tucked behind the reception desk.

Everywhere else, there was chaos. People ran around and puddles of raspberry jelly were splodged all over the place. There were angry parents and upset children  – and a queue of very disappointed people outside, who hadn't even got into the pool yet.

Wizard Beano nodded knowingly. *Food spells often go wrong,* he thought to himself.

Charlie thought it was hilarious. In fact, if kids' dirty hands and feet hadn't been in the massive pool of jelly, an afternoon jelly feast would have been a scrumptious way to spend the rest of the day!

Wizard Beano swiftly introduced himself to Diablo and, at lightning speed, waved his magic wand. His standard, 'Abracadabra' worked a treat.

'Abracadabra'

For a second, everything fell silent. Then, Diablo found himself catapulted back to the spot by the window where he'd been standing before he cast his spell.

Looking through the glass, he saw children playing in the pool, where the water was completely normal.

As Diablo sighed with relief, the bully boys from school, who had made fun of him the day before, suddenly turned round and left. Apparently, one of them had forgotten his swim suit ... Wizard Beano gave Diablo a wink.

A short while later, Diablo, Charlie and Wizard Beano sat down in a café. Diablo sat on a chair, while Charlie and the wizard, being very small, perched on top of the table. None of the grown-ups in the café could see them, of course. However, just to make absolutely sure, as if by magic, a drink of orange juice and a tasty flapjack appeared on the table next to the menu. These were treats for Diablo, but they were also useful for very small beings to hide behind.

Diablo hadn't realised how hungry he was. He gulped down some juice and ate half the flapjack in one bite. But he made sure to leave enough so that his new friends could stay hidden.

'How long have you been interested in magic?' asked Wizard Beano.

'Over a year now,' Diablo said proudly.

Wizard Beano watched as the hungry boy devoured some more flapjack.

'It takes a lot of energy and brain power to be a successful magician,' he explained. 'It takes patience and practice. A healthy body and mind. Eating and drinking regularly is essential.'

The wizard knew that being 'hangry' (both hungry and angry) was often a reason why mistakes were made.

Diablo thought of all the times he'd skipped breakfast and lunch, and hadn't bothered with anything to drink. His mam had constantly reminded him but he'd ignored her.

That was when Wizard Beano had an idea. 'I could teach you how to do magic, Diablo,' he suggested. He certainly didn't want to see the same mess again that he'd had to sort out earlier.

'But there is one condition,' the wizard went on. 'You must have eaten your meals before trying any magic spells. And along with your spell book, you must carry a water bottle and remember to drink from it.'

Diablo had heard of the mighty Wizard Beano and was so excited to be having his first proper magic lesson with him. He couldn't wait. He took notice of the wizard's advice too. And even though he'd eaten some flapjack, he already felt rather hungry.

Wizard Beano and Diablo agreed on when they would meet up, and Charlie suggested that perhaps at a weekend, Diablo could come on an adventure with them. Again, the condition was that he ate and drank regularly. Being magic, Wizard Beano knew that was the best way for Diablo to look after himself.

On the way back home later, Charlie and Wizard Beano began to feel hungry too.

'What would you like for tea?' Wizard Beano asked.

Charlie's eyes lit up. 'Jelly and ice cream, please,' they said. 'Although … perhaps not raspberry flavour today … if it's all the same to you …'

FOXY AND THE FAMILY TREE

Wizard Beano got up early every morning, when the sun came up. He had eventually come to terms with the fact that Charlie, who had moved in with him, was not an early riser. So they'd agreed that half past seven was the time they would both start the day.

However, that didn't stop Wizard Beano from creeping outside to have a few hours to himself before Charlie got up. He loved to watch a young fox, who visited the garden, play on the metal swing there.

Joseph Senior used to work in the shipyard and had built the swing for his children. It was later used by his grandchildren. He had made it from pieces of metal and some poles, and added chains and a wooden seat. It was a very solid swing. It needed to be to have survived this long, as it had been swung on over the years by lots of children and grown-ups.

This was where Foxy loved to swing too, at the end of the night.

One morning, Wizard Beano found him there once again. The sight of him made the wizard feel sad because Foxy always seemed to be in the garden on his own. He was never with any family or friends.

What Wizard Beano didn't know, however, was what the young fox kept in the garden shed.

The shed had been there for a number of years. It was well looked after, smartly painted and, most importantly, it was watertight.

The shed was used as a workplace, a study and an inventing space. It always looked to be a hive of activity. Joseph Senior also used it as a hiding place when he wanted a little quiet time!

There was a penknife on the bench, which was used to sharpen a well-worn pencil. There was an old drawing board, too, that Jeff used to use. Everything in that shed was made to last, just like the swing.

Foxy had managed to find a way into the shed each evening without being found out. He would work there in the dead of night. Then, as dawn broke, he would pack everything away neatly, so no one would notice.

He had rolls of maps, piles of pictures and lots of ideas.

What was most interesting was his Foxy family tree. To the untrained eye, all the foxes on the chart looked exactly the same. However, each fox actually had distinctly different markings.

Foxy's plans were nearly complete. He felt nervous but excited. He knew that in a few days, he would be ready for his adventure: to go and meet his family and perhaps make some new friends along the way. Even though Foxy quite liked his own company, the thought of meeting other foxes was wonderful.

'Hello,' said Wizard Beano from a branch of the cherry tree.

Foxy looked up, a shocked expression on his face.

He has about to leap off the swing and run away when Wizard Beano whispered, 'Abracadabra!'

The spell worked perfectly. It calmed Foxy down enough for Wizard Beano to jump into the garden and up onto the metal support of the swing. From there, he was able to reassure Foxy that he meant him no harm.

Foxy quickly felt quite chilled and relaxed, and somehow magical. Chatting away to Wizard Beano, he explained what his plans were for the next few days.

In the back of his mind, however, he couldn't help thinking, *What's happened? I've never had a long conversation like this with anyone before.*

But Foxy had to admit to himself that it did feel quite good to be able to share his plans and ideas, and to show the wizard his map.

In fact, it felt so good that he even agreed to meet up again with Wizard Beano the following morning.

Wizard Beano had some thoughts on their meeting too. 'I need to show Charlie the shed,' he said to himself. 'It's so organised and tidy. It could teach Charlie a thing or two.'

The next morning, Foxy went through the family tree with Wizard Beano. He explained that he'd located the areas he needed to visit to find his family, and following the river was very important.

He was interested in history too, and said he'd love to visit some of the places further down the river towards the sea. When he'd listened to the children as they played in the garden, Foxy had heard them say they'd seen dolphins.

Wizard Beano was getting just as excited. Whenever he'd visited the seaside to help with any problems or mishaps, he'd never seen dolphins. He'd heard people giggling, and oohing and ahhing as they played in the sand and jumped in the waves. But when he looked out to sea – nothing. No dolphins in sight. Not even a fin.

Perhaps this was his time too.

'Foxy,' Wizard Beano began, 'may Charlie and I please join you on your journey? It would be exciting to have an adventure all together.'

Foxy looked surprised. Then thoughtful. Then pleased. 'Yes,' the little fox said. 'That would be very nice.'

I haven't even left yet, he thought to himself, *and I've made two new friends already.*

Wizard Beano hurried back to the hollow in the cherry tree.

'Charlie,' he said, 'you must start to think about your outfit for tomorrow. We need to leave early in the morning and we'll be out on an adventure all day.' But even though he'd told Charlie, Wizard Beano knew he'd have to keep reminding them.

The next morning, all three adventurers gathered in the garden beside the swing.

Wizard Beano stared at Charlie with a disapproving look in his eye and shook his head. The backpack Charlie carried was huge. As well as a spade and a bucket hanging from the shoulder strap, it was stuffed with spare clothes.

'Well,' said Charlie, 'we're going on a journey. I thought I might need a change of outfits.'

Foxy made sure he had his map carefully rolled up and tucked away. Then off they set.

The first part of the trip involved making their way down to the riverside and heading towards the Spire Bridge. With the help of the carefully drawn map – and a little magic – they arrived in no time.

On one side, at the end of the main road, was the entrance gate to the old shipyard where Joseph Senior used to work. The travellers were pleased to see that the yard had been lovingly rebuilt and brought back to life. On the other side of the river, there were lots of shops and garages. The place bustled with activity.

Looking down the river, the three friends could see other bridges further along. They were amazed how different they all were.

The first was the Alexander Bridge. It was old and black, and looked in need of a good scrub or a fresh coat of paint. The travellers could tell it had been around for a long time and had seen the industrial age on the river.

35

The next bridge was the railway bridge that carried the Metro and other trains. Then there was the arch of the Town Bridge. Here, their eyes naturally followed the bend in the River Wear. But on the left, they could still catch a glimpse of the Stadium of Light.

They continued on their way, until Foxy said, 'We must be nearly at our next destination.' He pulled out the map and laid it on the ground.

The river bank on the left, before the Glass Centre, was where some of Foxy's family lived.

Foxy had discovered that many foxes lived near the river – urban foxes, existing alongside people and industrial areas quite happily. The fox lair he was looking for was on the bank itself, near the campus of the university.

Charlie was growing more and more excited. 'I've got an idea,' they said. 'While you look for your family, Wizard Beano and I will go exploring – if that's all right with you, Foxy,' they added.

Foxy agreed, so Charlie and the wizard hurried off to do some adventuring of their own.

Looking up at the Glass Centre, Charlie said, 'This glass building looks interesting. Plenty of places to climb!'

Before Wizard Beano could stop them, they'd run up towards the roof.

'Wow!' Charlie cried. 'You can walk on the glass ceiling!'

Wizard Beano blinked and thought, *Well, I only hope it's thick enough …*

Charlie then began to jump up and down on the ceiling, which made Wizard Beano feel more than a little anxious.

'Come away, Charlie,' he said.

'Why?' asked Charlie. 'Are you scared?' And a little smirk crossed their face.

'Of course I'm not scared,' scoffed the wizard.

But that wasn't actually true. Even with all his magic, Wizard Beano still felt a bit dizzy when he looked down through the glass at the people far below.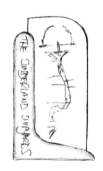

Meanwhile, Foxy chatted with other foxes on the river bank. He showed them his family tree and hoped so much they'd be able to help. All he wanted was to meet a member of his family, and soon. He'd worked so hard on this project, making plans, creating a map and finding out all about his ancestors.

However, by the time he met up with Charlie and Wizard Beano again, Foxy was beginning to think he'd done the wrong thing. Perhaps trying to find his family was a silly idea. None of the foxes he'd talked to had been able to help him.

'Let's go for a walk,' his two friends said both together.

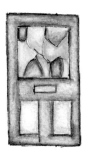

So they followed the river and found a pretty path around the harbour, where there was artwork and a stone bookcase, and even a beautiful, coloured-glass door.

Wizard Beano had been told that, in the harbour, there was a very magical place. If nothing else, he hoped visiting it would cheer Foxy up and help him to feel less disappointed.

The magical place was called 'North Dock Tufa'. It was a petrified cave, created out of seashells, complete with stalactites and stalagmites.

'North Dock Tufa' was a bit of a mouthful, but Wizard Beano could feel the magic as they got closer.

Just before they reached the beautiful display, Foxy saw some foxes run up the hill near the harbour. When they spotted him, they turned back.

'Glad we found you,' one of the foxes said. 'We heard you were looking for us.'

Foxy could hardly believe his eyes – and they grew bigger and rounder when he noticed the markings on the tail of the biggest fox.

'I was … I mean, I am,' he began. 'And I think you must be my cousin!'

As Foxy spoke, a huge smile spread across his face. Moments later, they were all hugging and nipping and rolling around doing foxy things.

Wizard Beano smiled too. 'I knew I could feel magic,' he said.

'See you soon!' the two pals called, as they left Foxy with his new-found family and headed towards the beach.

They found some wonderfully coloured shells. Heading on a little further to look for sea glass, Wizard Beano heard families all around him, oohing and aahing.

All of a sudden, he stopped still. He'd spotted something. Something he hadn't expected to see.

'Well, I never,' he said, as he watched some dolphins breach in the middle of the river, heading out to sea, between the piers at Roker.

'Quickly, Charlie!' he said. 'This never happens to me. Let's get a better look.'

With that, Wizard Beano pulled Charlie with him up into the air. There, they had a bird's eye view of the pier, the children and the huge pod of dolphins.

Wizard Beano chuckled joyfully. 'Finally, when people ask, "Have you seen all the dolphins playing at Roker?" I'll be able to say, "YES"!'

Back in Hastings Hill the next morning, when Wizard Beano slipped out from the cherry tree, he noticed that Foxy wasn't on the swing.

Probably too busy with his family, the wizard thought happily. *What a truly magical day we had.*

A week later, Wizard Beano and Charlie were getting itchy feet. They'd realised how much they'd enjoyed their adventure with Foxy and how exciting it would be to go travelling again.

Looking thoughtful, Charlie asked, 'What is it?'

'What's what?' asked Wizard Beano.

'You know,' replied Charlie. 'The yellow train thing. We saw it on the railway bridge over the river.'

'Ah,' said Wizard Beano. 'That's the Metro. It's a train that takes people all over the North East.'

Charlie's eyes sparkled. 'Then let's go for a ride!' they said.

And that's exactly what they both did.

So, if you're a child, do keep your eyes wide open, won't you? Because the next thing you see might be Wizard Beano and Charlie, hanging on to the front of a Metro carriage and shrieking out ... 'NEWCASTLE – here we come!'

About the Author

Paula Fowler lives in East Boldon in the North East of England. After working in the world of banking and travel, her career was cut short by a stage 4 cancer diagnosis.

Not wanting to let that define her, Paula has continued to use all her skills, experiences and creativity to help and support others.

The latter part of 2021 brought Paula and author/artist Kylie Dixon together again, after meeting at work. Paula asked Kylie to work on a commission piece for the family's new addition – a great-grandchild. It was through this commission that Paula realised she had to share the story of Wizard Beano, a character told of in bedtime tales within the Fowler household.

The ideas that had been locked away came to life. With new stories and fresh characters, Wizard Beano was reborn.

This is Paula's first book, and she has plans to write more. If Paula has learnt anything in life, especially as she goes through her cancer prognoses, it's about the power of friendship and being kind, and the need to look after our surroundings and, importantly, ourselves.

About the Illustrator

Kylie Dixon is an author, artist and illustrator from Seaham – you can find out more about her and her work in her Facebook group, The Magical World of Mushroom Marvellous. Her beautiful, whimsical style lends itself perfectly to this book. Kylie took Paula's ideas and put them skilfully onto paper, bringing all of these magical characters to life more vividly than Paula thought possible. Her delightful illustrations have made this into a truly special book, which will leave an important legacy for the Fowler family.